I0621023

Arctic Adagio

DJ Cockburn

AnnorlundaBooks

Cover design by Nerine Dorman.

Editing services from Nerine Dorman.

Published in the United States by Annorlunda Books.

Queries: info@annorlundaenterprises.com

First Edition

ISBN-13: 978-1-944354-47-3

Arctic Adagio

When your job is to babysit the richest people in the world, being able to keep a straight face is as important as being able to recognize an armed anarchist. The Yefimovs were straining my straight face to the limit with swimming costumes so tiny they may as well have been naked. The heated pool produced a cloud of vapor where it met the Arctic air, but not enough of it for my liking.

I could still see the Yefimovs.

"Global warming is a truly marvelous thing," Arkadi Yefimov was saying to me. "To think only a few decades ago, the sea beneath our hull was solid ice."

The aurora sent reflections chasing across the pool, staining their mismatched bodies across the spectrum. He looked like an elderly hippo, too bloated and arthritic to do anything but wallow. She acted the role of the trophy wife, long limbs wrapped around him and her blonde head nodding in time with his words.

"It must have been such a waste," she said. "What would be the use of a solar storm if we couldn't get to the best place to see it?"

"Exactly," he said. "The wisdom of my grandfather's generation wasn't appreciated in his day, but we can pay tribute to it now."

I huddled in my parka. "Yes sir."

Before I was head of security on board the *Ayn Rand*, I'd spent twenty-six years in London's Metropolitan Police. The Met had taught me the value of those two words.

"But I didn't ask you here to discuss my family history," said Yefimov. "My son wishes to fire a Rarden on his twelfth birthday."

"I... Well... A thirty-millimeter cannon isn't a toy, sir."

"You will make sure he is safe."

I should have seen it coming. We had the Rardens because a ship full of trillionaires who refused any nationality offered a tempting target for pirates. If our guests had seen them smash a few skiffs to matchwood, it only made their children more eager to play with them.

"When's his birthday, sir?"

"Next week."

"I'll see what I can do."

Yefimov returned his attention to the dancing sky. I'd been put out of his mind.

"See you do, Superintendent Harme," said his wife.

No woman marries a man half a century older than her unless she's jumping a few social classes. Lydia Yefimova's glare showed she'd yet to get the hang of authority. People born to it, like her husband, didn't bother reminding me of it.

My comm chirped.

"Excuse me," I said.

"We've lost the cameras on decks three, five and six." I couldn't place his voice, so it must have been someone new.

"Lost? What do you mean lost?"

"Lost… I mean, they're dead."

Tech wasn't my department, so there was nothing I could do about it, and Surveillance could keep me informed on the comm.

Yefimova looked as if she had more to say.

"I'm coming down," I said.

I left the Yefimovs to the aurora that generations of carbon baron Yefimovs had opened to them. The moment I entered the superstructure, the *Ayn Rand* hit me with a blast of heat. I stripped off my parka as I waited for the elevator.

In Surveillance, a barrage of obscenities told me the IT head was already at her station. Since joining the *Ayn Rand*, Fern Hanway had gained more than the couple of kilos that proper meals put on most of us. I thought they suited her but kept such observations to myself. The *Ayn Rand* could take no credit for a vocabulary that would have set laziest constables I'd ever bollocked to scribbling notes. She'd learned it a few miles down the River Thames from my own patch.

Fern seemed to think she was swearing under her breath, but the duty officer was devoting far more concentration to the wall of screens than was warranted when half of them were blank. Nguyen, that was his name. It had been his voice I couldn't place on the comm. He'd only joined us three weeks ago, when we visited Haiphong. His English was as excellent as it needed to be for anyone who wanted to climb out of the precariat, but by his expression, Fern was introducing him to meanings he'd never before contemplated.

Fern broke off to look at me. "I sodding well told them this would happen."

"Yes," I said. "You did."

"Wire up a ship like a cat's cradle and go watch the pretty lights." She turned back to the screen. "Oh no, we're rich, we can pay off a solar storm…"

"Would you like a coffee, sir?" asked Nguyen.

I didn't, but I accepted because his embarrassment hurt to watch. Nguyen was in his mid-twenties, about the same age as Geoff. Was it my curse that every superficial resemblance reminded me of the son I hadn't seen for two years? Nguyen's eagerness to please was nothing like the resentment that had furrowed Geoff's face the last time I saw him.

I told Nguyen to put the feed from the cameras that were working on the screens. Most showed empty corridors. Some were tinted blue and green where they picked up a little of the sky.

Surveillance was part of the compromise the Kurata Corporation offered its guests. They wanted to buy absolute liberty for themselves but unless they could afford the whole ship, they would have to share their liberty with people they had no reason to trust. That was why the residence contract was so comprehensive that it had a clause prohibiting cannibalism, and why the *Ayn Rand*'s cameras covered everything but the cabins.

"Thanks, Nguyen." I took the coffee he offered me. "I don't need to tell you our guests don't need to know about this. We wouldn't want to worry their pretty heads with our problems, would we?"

"I understand, sir."

Fern stood. "Right, spanners and screwdrivers time. Nguyen, stay here and keep an eye on what we've got left. Sir, would you call a couple of electricians? I'll start at port thirty-two on deck four… What?"

Nguyen was waving at a screen showing one of the Rarden ports. The psychedelic sky silhouetted the twin barrels while the wide-angle lens bent the edge of the hull into a curve. What had got Nguyen's attention was the figure in a hooded parka carrying someone across his shoulders.

Fern and I both looked at the door control console.

"The door to number four Rarden's open," she said.

The hooded figure threw the body over the side.

I hit the general alarm. The siren usually meant a pirate attack, but it would send everyone to their cabins or duty stations where they could be accounted for.

Nguyen was already on the comm to the bridge. "Man overboard! Port side!"

I was on my own comm, trying to sound calm as I diverted securitati running to their posts to the corridors around number four Rarden.

As the engine vibration faded, I knew it was pointless. Whoever went over the side would have been sucked under the hull. The only mercy was that the Arctic Ocean was cold enough to kill them with hypothermia before they drowned. Meanwhile, Nguyen was throwing switches, looking for a live camera that covered any of the corridors near number four, but the screens stayed blank. Whoever had thrown the body had anticipated the search and planned an escape route, so I wasn't surprised when none of the securitati reported anyone scurrying down a corridor looking furtive.

"Nguyen," I said.

"Sir?"

"Next time you see a murder in progress, you have my permission to interrupt your superior officers. In fact, that's an order."

The Met taught us drill for the passing out parade at Hendon Police College, but since then I'd used it fewer than a dozen times and had always been out of step. Yet standing before Captain Espinosa's desk, I found myself at a rough approximation of attention. I was confident I wasn't at fault, so I forced myself into a more relaxed posture.

"Barber's *Adagio for Strings*," I said.

Espinosa frowned, as if noticing the music in his cabin for the first time.

"Music helps me to think too," I said.

Espinosa's blink betrayed an urge to ask how a plodding policeman gained an appreciation of classical music. It would be an equally pertinent question to a Filipino who first went to sea as a semi-literate deckhand. Being head of security gave me access to personnel files, and being a nosey copper by nature, I'd read them.

"Good," he said. "You're going to be doing some thinking. You're absolutely sure the victim was Tanjiro Kurata?"

"I'm afraid so. He's the only person unaccounted for."

"Hm."

"So, whatever you're thinking of telling me about him, sir, I need to know it. It'll stay between you, me and the walls."

"Bulkheads."

"You, me and the bulkheads, then."

Espinosa glanced around the bulkheads, or walls, or whatever they were called.

"Let's go to the bridge," he said.

"Sir, I promise we're not bugging you."

"I'm sure you're not."

He had a point. If the Kurata Corporation had installed a separate surveillance system for the guests to keep tabs on the senior officers, I wouldn't know about it.

Perhaps I'd adopted the paranoia I was paid to indulge because I'd brought my parka with me in case the conversation took this turn.

The wind scouring the open wing of the bridge dropped the temperature to well below freezing, but it reassured me even as it flayed my cheeks. If we were being bugged, anyone listening would have to spend more time cleaning the recording than a casual eavesdropper would bother with.

Espinosa nodded off the side of the ship, or the beam as he would have called it. "I want you to see our shadow."

To the south, the gray sun had reached its zenith of a few degrees above the horizon, giving a milky tint to the overcast sky. It took me a moment to see straight edges in the gray sea. There was a ship out there, about two kilometers away, although I didn't trust my estimation of distances over water. As I got my eye in, I made out the gun and missile tubes on the bow and the red splash of the flag flying over the tangle of radar masts.

"Japanese," I said. "Let me guess, they're here to collect whoever ditched Kurata and take him to where his family can flay him alive."

"No," said Espinosa. "They're here for Kurata himself."
"Should've brought a sub, then."

I must have interviewed too many suspects because it had become a habit not to prompt someone when they wanted me to.

"Rex, do you know why the Kuratas build their ships in Japan?"

"Because it's one of the last countries left with a working shipyard."

"Yes, but why is that?"

I said nothing.

"Because it's the last country with a government that isn't in the pockets of people like our guests. Their judiciary's still independent enough to hold manufacturers to their contracts, so they make components to contract specifications." He closed a hand around the bridge rail as though it was the shoulder of a friend. "They could have had her built in France or Russia or Brazil for half the cost, but she'd have sunk under us by now."

"If you're saying regulation's good for industry," I said, "I can see why you don't want our guests to hear you."

"Oh, all our guests know it, which is why they trust Japanese-built ships. They'd rather take their chances among the precariat than in a ship built without regulation."

"Some of them spent decades lobbying against regulation."

He waved at the penthouses in the superstructure. "Which is why the Japanese government knows none of them would think twice about bribing their politicians to vote down inconvenient regulations. Our guests didn't get rich by taking the long view. That's why the Japanese lock up anyone who tries to bribe their legislators. Even if they're from a family as rich as the Kuratas."

"I don't think I like where this is going."
"You shouldn't. Because according to the message I received from that frigate, Tanjiro Kurata tried it."

"That problem seems to have solved itself."

I'd wondered why Kurata was a guest on the *Ayn Rand* rather than at Kurata headquarters in Tokyo. The sort of poor judgment that would put his family on the wrong side of the Japanese authorities would explain why they wanted him at a safe distance. It seemed the distance hadn't been as safe as they'd hoped.

"Except they're still shadowing us." He nodded at the frigate. "They haven't said any more, but there they are."

Espinosa turned to me, his eyes framed by his hood. His meaning was plain. The Japanese authorities found it too convenient that Tanjiro Kurata went over the side of one of his family's ships a few hours before a frigate turned up to arrest him.

The Kurata Corporation's business was based on our guests believing their collective wealth bought them more protection than any national flag. I hoped they'd noticed the frigate because while their influence had stopped us being boarded, the frigate hadn't gone away, and the distance it was keeping precisely calibrated the validity of our guests' belief.

"As he's gone over the side, they can think what they like," I said.

Espinosa faced ahead.

"Meanwhile, we're ordered to Murmansk, where the whole crew will be replaced."

"Sir?" Had the wind had distorted his words?

"I'm disobeying my orders by telling you. The first you're supposed to know about it is when the new security detail comes aboard and forces everyone ashore."

"Why Murmansk?"

"You were a detective, Rex. I'm sure you can work it out."

I could. Yefimov and his ilk might have warmed the Arctic Circle, but only a climatologist would care about a difference measured in degrees below freezing. The people of Murmansk had only cared about that when OPEC priced heating oil above the precariat's budget. They'd left to try their luck in the slums sprawling around every city that wasn't frozen or parched.

We wouldn't last a week.

Tanjiro Kurata's family would ensure his murderer was punished by punishing anyone who might have done it. If they were assuming it was a crew member rather than a guest, it wouldn't be the first time they'd made the assumptions that were best for business. I folded my arms around my parka's bulk. It had been issued by the Kurata Corporation, so they'd take it away when they beached me in Murmansk.

"I take it that's your way of motivating me to find the murderer," I said.

"No. It's the Kurata family's way. My way is more simple. I'm ordering you to find the murderer."

"Sir, you realize…"

"That our security is structured to protect the guests, not investigate murders. Yes, I do. My order stands."

"I'll remember that when I'm watching you sail away from Murmansk."

"I'll be ashore with you."

"Sir?"

"The Kuratas are excellent motivators. They were even thorough enough to remind me my son and daughter live in the port workers' compound in Manila, and they'll force them out if I don't keep these orders to myself."

I hoped my parka was bulky enough to hide my shaking shoulders. If the Kuratas were threatening Espinosa's kids, Hendon Police College wasn't going to give Geoff much protection.

"How long do we have?"

"We'll be in Murmansk in three days. I told them we have a reactor problem, but I couldn't cut our speed any more without risking more motivation."

"They must be sure it's one of the crew and not a guest?"

Espinosa turned to face me. "I don't mean to tell you your business, but hadn't you better get started?"

"With respect, sir, that question was me getting started."

"Of course. Forgive me."

Espinosa had put a lot of trust in me by telling me about Murmansk. I wished I hadn't repaid him by making him apologize, but I wasn't having a conversation with my commanding officer now. I was questioning a witness.

"I did ask," he said. "If they suspect one of the guests, they weren't dropping any hints."

"Thank you, sir."

"You suspect a guest?"

"Not yet."

I returned to Surveillance, where Fern was flicking through the cameras she'd spent the night repairing. She was at home in a swivel chair surrounded by screens. I wondered how long she'd last in Murmansk.

She looked up. "Hello sir. Coffee's hot."

"Thanks. Not now."

I'd spent the past eight hours coordinating fruitless searches for any sort of evidence. I'd drunk enough coffee to make my stomach churn.

Fern shrugged and held up a circuit board with a charred hole in the middle.

"Timed charge?" I asked.

"Looks like it. Thirteen circuits altogether. It looked random, but it covered a lot of ways to and from number four Rarden."

"Any idea how he got into the bay? Did he know the door code?"

"Looks like it."

I swallowed a curse. That put my securitati in the frame, so I couldn't depend on them in the investigation.

"Sir," said Nguyen, who was watching the monitors on the wall. "Sorry, but you said I should speak if…"

My stomach lurched. I scanned the monitors for what had caught Nguyen's attention.

"I was thinking, sir. It was a big coincidence the cameras were sabotaged during a solar storm."

"It wasn't a *coincidence*." I spoke more harshly than I'd intended, relieved no one else was being murdered. I wanted to shout at him, call him a fool, vent the frustration of the past few hours. I forced a level tone into my voice. "Everyone knew the storm was coming. That's why we're freezing our arses off up here. So our guests can watch the aurora. If the cameras went down without a clear reason, we'd have called the securitati immediately. As it was, he waited until everyone was on the observation deck watching the aurora."

Nguyen looked ready to burst into tears. I saw Geoff in him again and pushed away the thought. Stray thoughts of my son would distract me and worse, would prejudice me in favor of whoever evoked them.

It was a way of thinking I hadn't used since I'd left the Met. Regaining it felt like putting on a pair of shoes that were perfectly worn in to my feet.

I took a deep breath. "It was a good thought, Nguyen. Please tell me about anything else you come up with. It's the only way we'll find the ditcher."

"Sir?"

I shrugged. "It's as good a name as any."

"Yes sir."

Nguyen's tone told me I did impatience better than conciliation.

"Sir?" Fern had an account ledger called up on her screen. "You'll want to see this."

"Just a moment. Nguyen, when does your watch finish?"

"Three hours ago, sir. My relief is checking the camera circuits for any more explosives."

"Good man, but you should get some sleep."

"I'm fine, sir, I can…"

"You're relieved, Nguyen. We've got Surveillance, and I need you alert when you're next on duty."

"I… Yes sir. Thank you, sir."

I watched him leave, thinking he was no better suited to Murmansk than Fern.

Or me.

I looked over Fern's shoulder.

"Best if you keep anything you find between us," I said. "Murder has a way of becoming gossip, and the ditcher will be paying attention."

"Okay. But look at this."

"What is it?"

"It's the computer your team collected from Kurata's penthouse. We're looking at the financial transactions that passed through it."

"Are you supposed to be seeing that?"
"Sir, if the Kuratas only wanted their IT people to see what they're contracted to, they wouldn't hire such good ones."

I couldn't argue with that.

"Call me Rex."

"Kurata didn't have much in his own name. His family paid his rent here and sent him an allowance of a hundred and forty grand a month, which is peanuts on this boat."

It was several times either of our salaries, but I took her point.

"Three months ago, he takes a payment of a hundred and twenty million yuan from Daniel McNamara, who lives on the same deck as him.

"McNamara. I think I'll have that coffee after all."

I filled a mug and sat down.

"McNamara started as a hedge fund manager," said Fern. "Five years out of Harvard Business School he'd made enough to be a major investor on his own account. He got out of the States before the Fragmentation. Hasn't looked back since."

The guests' files were something else she wasn't supposed to have access to but I nodded, remembering the week I'd spent on the *Ayn Rand*'s hovercraft with McNamara and two securitati. McNamara had wanted to get his hands on a Zulu spear and shield while the *Ayn Rand* was in Durban. After days of blasting over the cratered remains of roads and through towns abandoned when rivers ran dry, we ended up in a squatter camp beside the trickle remaining of the Mpumalanga River. Our enquiries led us to an old man sitting outside his shack, who greeted us with a fit of coughing from the hovercraft's dust.

"You get Zulu spear and shield?" McNamara shouted at him. "Me want!"

A woman I took to be his daughter jogged up with a tin of water. The old man waved her away.

"Keep it for the children." He stifled his coughs and stood. If he stood less than straight, it stole nothing from a dignity undiminished by poverty. "I used to be a professor of literature at the University of KwaZulu-Natal. There's no need to shout."

"I hear you have a Zulu spear and shield." McNamara showed no contrition, but he moderated his tone to the conversational.

"I have."

He led us into his shack and rummaged under his bed frame. The cowhide on the shield was faded in places, but the spear looked as though age had only made it straighter and stronger. I was embarrassed to be poring over his possessions without knowing his name, but it wasn't my place to take the lead.

"How old are these?"

"I don't know exactly. The pattern on the shield belongs to the uNokenke regiment."

"The uNokenke?" asked McNamara. "They were at Isandlwana in eighteen seventy-nine."

The man smiled. "That's right. Not many people have heard of that now. My grandfather inherited these. He would wave the spear when the apartheid government tried to disarm the Zulu in the nineteen eighties."

"I'll give you five hundred yuan for both of them."

The man's daughter appeared in the doorway. She must have been listening from outside.

"You can't sell them," she said. "They've been in the family for two centuries."

"The children are hungry, Beatrice." He turned back to McNamara. "But they're worth ten thousand."

McNamara spent half an hour beating him down to two thousand. He didn't notice when I couldn't stand it anymore and slipped outside. Beatrice looked like a formidable character, so I unloaded our food and water and asked her to give it to whoever needed it most. Her thanks cut far deeper than the contempt I deserved would have done.

I waited until the camp had vanished behind the hovercraft's dust cloud before I told McNamara we'd need another supply run from the *Ayn Rand*'s helicopter. He didn't look up from caressing the spear. "Call it in, then."

The supply run cost fifty thousand yuan.

In Surveillance, I put aside the coffee. The memory made me feel queasy enough. I'd summoned it to ask myself a question: would

McNamara ditch Kurata for a hundred and twenty million yuan? A lot of people think about murder and many get as far as planning it, but not many are capable of carrying it out, and even fewer of keeping their mouths shut afterward. I'd put several behind bars because they'd gone for a few beers and told half a pub what they'd done. One of them told me he couldn't understand why he'd been so stupid. All I could tell him was murder does that to people.

There's no way to tell if someone can pull off cold-blooded murder. Most people don't know themselves unless they find something worth murdering for.

"Anything else in there?" I asked Fern.

"Not yet. I'll keep at it."

"Good, but call Nguyen's relief and get a couple of hours' sleep first. You don't want to miss something because you're dozing off."

"I'm fine."

"Don't make me order you just after I've told you to use my first name."

I left before she could reply. Hopefully she'd see sense if I wasn't there to argue with.

I took the elevator up to the superstructure and pressed the buzzer outside McNamara's penthouse. The speaker made his reply sound far away, although he was only on the other side of the wall. Or bulkhead as Espinosa would want me to call it.

"I didn't order anything," he said.

"I'm not room service. This is Rex Harme. Security. I'd appreciate a moment of your time, Mr. McNamara."

"Harme?"

Sometimes I missed my warrant card.

"We spent a week in the hovercraft, tracking down the Zulu spear and shield."

The door slid open. McNamara's graying hair needed a trim. His jeans and T-shirt wouldn't have been out of place in some of the sink estates I'd only been to with a busload of backup. When I started this job, I'd had to get used to how ordinary a trillionaire could look.

"You want to see my weapons collection, I guess," he said.

"Actually…"

"Everyone does."

He slid open another door. Lights flicked on, revealing a room the size of his office filled with a paraphernalia of pain. The walls were hung with swords and muskets. Colt and Webley revolvers shared display cases with sub-machine guns and assault rifles of types I used to put in evidence bags.

I felt a prick of shame when I recognized the spear and shield.

"This is a particular favorite." McNamara removed a Luger pistol from a bracket. "Belonged to Himmler. Gathered as evidence at the end of the Second World War and got locked in a cupboard."

He held it out as though it would be a privilege to touch it. His reverence told me he'd never seen what blades and bullets did to the human body. I had. Every time I drew a gun from the armory, it tied a knot in my stomach.

I folded my arms. "How did you get it?"

McNamara shrugged. "The German government went bankrupt after they cut taxes. I bought it from a clerk who hadn't been paid for six months. Usual story. Sort of thing that was good for you. Most of us did well out of cuts like that, so their loss got you your job."

By *us*, he didn't mean him and me. He meant him and other trillionaires.

"I'm deeply grateful." There was no point in telling him how much I missed being a proper copper. "Perhaps we could go back to your office. I'd like to ask a few questions about Tanjiro Kurata."

"Kurata? The young idiot who got himself thrown overboard?"

"That's him."

McNamara put back the Luger and led me to his office. He sat at his computer and waved at the window facing the Japanese frigate.

"Something to do with them?" he asked.

"Something."

The sky behind the frigate was slate gray. The weather was about to turn nasty.

McNamara was tapping his keyboard. I was a poor audience, so he'd lost interest in me. I wondered if he was sourcing his next weapon or refining trading algorithms to scoop another few million yuan of the world's wealth into his bank accounts. I thought about going back into his collection and stamping on a crossbow to get his attention.

I sat down. "Mr. McNamara, you paid Tanjiro Kurata a hundred and twenty million yuan a couple of months ago. May I ask why?"

His fingers froze, hovering over the keyboard. "How do you know that?"

"Kurata didn't trust his computer to keep his accounts secure. He wrote everything down in a paper ledger."

No point in telling him about Fern's sleuthing. McNamara must have believed me, because his fingers returned to the keyboard. I waited for an explanation, but he seemed to have forgotten I was there.

"It seems Kurata used the money to try to bribe several Japanese politicians," I said. "He wasn't very good at it, and the money's been seized by the Japanese authorities."

That made him pause. Not as long as when he thought his computer might not be secure. Longer than when I mentioned Kurata's death. I was getting a sense of McNamara's priorities.

"Hence our escort."

He nodded as he turned back to his computer, as though he'd fitted a piece into a jigsaw.

"Mr. McNamara," I said. "Did you know what Tanjiro Kurata was planning to do with the money?"

He stopped typing and looked me in the eye. "No. I thought I was investing in the Kurata Corporation's next ship."

For a man whose default attitude was indifference, unblinking honesty was overdoing it. He'd known he was underwriting a bribe.

I said nothing.

McNamara filled the silence. "I don't see that whatever Kurata was up to in Japan is any of your business. We're not under Japanese jurisdiction."

"We're not under any jurisdiction, but it's my business that someone killed a guest, and my experience is that it's never a waste of time to follow the money."

"I lent him some. Money followed."

The set of McNamara's shoulders told me I wouldn't get any more out of him without some sort of leverage, which I didn't have.

I stood up. "As you say, money followed. Thanks for your time."

He didn't look up. I returned to Surveillance and rolled my eyes to see Fern still there, even though the duty officer was now at the station Nguyen had vacated.

"Any luck?" There was an edge to Fern's voice.

I wondered if she'd found out we were going to be marooned in Murmansk. Was she tapping communication between Espinosa and the Kuratas? Paranoia was becoming a habit.

I shrugged. It was possible that McNamara and Kurata had fallen out over their scheme, but possibility was a long way from certainty, let alone evidence. "He likes things that hurt people. Other than that, who knows?"

Fern's shoulders sagged as she sighed.

"It was a place to start," I said. "Anything else?"

"No," she said. "Nothing abnormal. What will you do now?"

"What I told you to do. Sleep for a couple of hours. You should do the same, then go over everything again when you're a bit fresher."

"Right," she said. "Yes."

My answer seemed to drain her nervous energy. Her personnel file said she was forty-two, but she rose from her desk as if she had the joints of a woman twice her age.

I went back to my cabin. Before I lay down, I found myself looking at the computer built into my desk.

I couldn't use my communication allowance if I was beached in Murmansk.

A few minutes less sleep wouldn't matter much. I was tapping keys before I finished the thought, connecting to the London microwave net. The computer told me to wait. It had been so much easier when everyone could afford phones. I remembered when a call connected immediately because a provider who made you wait would lose your business to a competitor.

"Dad?" Geoff's voice came through the speakers.

"Hello, Geoff."

"It's past midnight here, Dad."

"Is it? Sorry, I lost track of time."

The speakers carried Geoff's sigh with the fidelity I'd expect from a manufacturer subcontracted by the Kuratas, as well as a few obscenities from the background.

"Geoff, I just wanted to —"

"Hang on, Dad."

I heard footsteps and the click of a door closing.

"I'm in a dorm, Dad. You just woke everyone up."

"I'm sorry."

"Right, I'm outside now. What is it?"

"I…"

Good question. Had my relationship with my son been this awkward before Carol died?

"I just wanted to know how things are for you, you know?"

"Couldn't it have waited until tomorrow? I spent fourteen hours doing riot control drills today, and it'll be the same tomorrow."

When I'd been at Hendon, riot control hadn't been a big part of the curriculum.

"I'm sorry. Some bad stuff went down today." That was as close to the truth as I dared over a link owned by the Kuratas. "You pass out in six weeks, right?"

"Five."

"Well, that's good."

"Dad, I may as well tell you. I'm leaving as soon as I pass out."

"What?"

"I said —"

"I know, I heard you, but you worked your arse off to get into Hendon."

"A black helmet's not right for me, Dad. I can't do what you did. They don't even throw people out for that anymore. They'd probably give you a medal now."

It was bad enough to be reminded why I was thrown out of the police. Worse that it came from my son.

"I didn't shoot her, Geoff. It was a constable on his first raid. He panicked."

"I know. You were thrown out because you ran the operation and used an unwarranted phone tap. Did any of them even have a weapon?"

This wasn't the conversation I'd wanted, but if I was going to be beached, I may not have another chance to tell him the truth. I hadn't told him before because I hadn't wanted to put him off joining the police. At least, that was what I'd told myself. Perhaps I just hadn't wanted to talk about it. It was one of many things that had fallen into the gap between Geoff and me.

"No. They didn't," I said. "When we went in, that girl grabbed a two-by-four they were using for their placards. It was dark. The constable thought it was a shotgun. In the enquiry, we called it a club but that was to cover him. It would have snapped over his helmet.

"And you took the fall for him?"

"I wasn't planning to, but I'd been asking questions nobody wanted to answer."

"You did?" Geoff sounded surprised. "Like what?"

"The sort of questions you're asking now. Why we'd started responding to protests by putting on the riot gear instead of basic crowd control. Why the Special Branch teams monitoring protest groups were bigger than the units investigating the protection rackets running outside the gated communities. Things I guess look normal now, but it wasn't like that when I joined."

"You weren't just a drone then? I mean—"

"No, Geoff, I wasn't just a drone."

Did Geoff's silence mean he was reconsidering his view of me? I dared hope.

"If that's true," he said, "you'll understand why I need to leave."

Of course I understood. That was the problem.

"It's not that I can't hack it," he said. "I can. I'm going to pass out, but then I'm done."

I almost asked why graduation mattered to him but stifled the question. Geoff's objection to the police might run deeper than he was saying. He might want to learn as much as he could and take it to a dissident group. If I could make that deduction, so could anyone listening. I wanted to change the subject before he made it any more obvious.

I forced myself to sound cheerful. "Well, I'm sure you know what you want. All I ask is that you think it over. Wait till you've passed out before you make any final decisions."

"I've already decided, Dad." If Geoff was in touch with a dissident group, they hadn't taught him anything about operational security. "I know why you wanted me in. You're afraid I'll end up in the precariat. I get it, Dad, I do, but I can't live my life based on what I'm afraid of."

The trouble with being twenty-two was that you weren't afraid of anything until it was in your face. No, that was unfair. If more of us had thought like Geoff when I was twenty-two, it might not be so dangerous for Geoff to think such thoughts now.

"Geoff, I admire your courage. In fact, I envy it, but let me tell you something. I work for the richest and most powerful people in the world. Thing is, they're all afraid. I protect them from the precariat, but what they're really afraid of is *becoming* the precariat. They're all a few bad investments from sliding down to the gated communities that have to keep paying governments to run countries for their benefit. Then a few more from being like us, people who get by because the rich pay us for what they need. And we do our jobs as best we can because we're one bad call away from the precariat, which is ninety percent of the world and full of people who want to show they can do our jobs better than us. That's how the world works, Geoff. That's why everyone's afraid, and that's why I'm asking you to think very, very carefully about the decision you're about to make."

If anyone was listening, I didn't think they'd object to me trying to tell Geoff to be part of the system they approved of. If they did, what were they going to do about it? Put me ashore in Murmansk?

"Right, Dad. I'll think about it."

I'd lost him.

"Do that."

"Look, Dad, it's like I said. Riot drill tomorrow. I need to sleep."

"Sure. Good to talk to you."

"You too. Bye."

He rang off.

I slumped on the bed and flipped on the sound system, which launched into the middle of the

Dvořák playlist I'd left it on. Perhaps it was Espinosa's inspiration that made me switch to Barber's *Adagio*. I wanted Barber's violins to lift my soul to where it could look down on the wreckage of itself. It took a composer as brilliant as Barber to make sense of the idea.

I fell asleep instead.

———◦———

My comm woke me. "It's Nguyen in Surveillance. Sorry to bother you, sir, but you said — "

"I know what I said. Do you have something?"

"Yes sir. I've been reviewing Mr. Kurata's movements in the last few weeks…"

Nguyen's words banished sleep and let in paranoia.

"Good man. I'll come up now."

I cut the call before he could give any details.

As I get older, I swear my joints rust as I sleep. I took the stairs rather than the elevator to Surveillance, trying to get some blood flowing around my brain before I had to use it. I must have needed it because I only noticed the *Ayn Rand*'s lively roll when my stiff knees nearly dropped me down a staircase. The bad weather I'd seen from McNamara's penthouse had arrived.

It was worth nearly breaking my neck because by the time I got to Surveillance, I was starting to see layers of information beneath the patchwork quilt of observations and impressions I'd been collecting. More importantly, I was seeing what didn't fit between them.

"Morning, Nguyen."

"Uh, good evening, sir," said Nguyen.

"Hm?" My brain wasn't working that well after all. I poured myself a coffee to get it in gear. Once a detective, always a detective. "What have you got?"

Nguyen tapped his keyboard. On the screen, an obese man left a penthouse and waddled down a corridor. The timestamp showed it was from three weeks ago.

"That's Arkadi Yefimov, isn't it?" I asked.

"Yes, that's his cabin, sir. Fifteen minutes later..."

Nguyen sent the time stamp blurring forward until a figure in a hoodie loped up the corridor. Precariat chic.

Nguyen slowed the recording as the figure paused outside Yefimov's door. The hoodie twitched both ways in a parody of furtiveness then slipped into Yefimov's penthouse.

"Kurata?" I asked.

"Yes sir, I traced him back to Mr. Kurata's penthouse. How did you know?"

"I *am* a detective, Nguyen."

"Sorry sir."

"Don't be. You wouldn't have called me if it was anyone else. Detective work is mostly grinding away at the information until something falls out, which is what you've been doing while I was asleep. That makes you the better detective right now."

"Thank you, sir."

It was going to take a while to persuade Nguyen to relax around me. My job was to make sure I'd be doing it on the *Ayn Rand* and not in Murmansk.

"I'll take a wild guess La Yefimova's still in there?"

"Yes sir."

"I'm guessing that's not the only time?" I asked.

"Seven times in the last month. That's as far back as I've got so far."

"That's enough to ask Yefimov some awkward questions."

Which could turn very awkward if he hadn't had Kurata killed. The Kurata Corporation had no policy on what we should do if we discovered such infidelities. They were as likely to fire us for co-operating as for refusing to co-operate with suspicious spouses. My own policy was to know as little as possible about such things. Especially when I was asked about them.

"Let's get Fern Hanway in here," I said.

She arrived looking as disheveled as I felt. Without her makeup, I could see the lines around her eyes. Fine by me. I like lines. They give me something to read.

Her lines etched deeper when Nguyen showed her Kurata sneaking into Yefimov's penthouse.

"According to guest records," I said, "Yefimov's seventy-eight, his wife's thirty, and Yefimov's got one of the biggest bar bills on the ship. She must get tired of the old piss-head, and Kurata wasn't short in the looks department."

Fern shook her head. "The man who threw Kurata over the side wasn't Yefimov. Yefimov couldn't carry Kurata. He can hardly carry himself."

"True, but Yefimov didn't have the code to the Rarden bay either. He could have bribed one of the securitati. Trillionaires don't get their own hands dirty."

"We don't know why Kurata was going to Yefimov's. He was probably just…"

"Just?"

"I don't know. Are you going to talk to Yefimov?"

"No need. I know who did it."

I wished I'd earned the looks that Fern and Nguyen were looking at me with. Knowing who had done it mattered less than knowing exactly what they'd done, and I wasn't there yet.

"What I need now is evidence to take to the Kuratas. I'm going to have the securitati search the superstructure as soon as I've drawn up a plan. Meanwhile, keep all the screens feeding from the superstructure. If anyone's moving around, I want to know about it."

Nguyen was switching camera feeds before I finished speaking.

"Fern," I said, "would you double check the camera circuits in the superstructure while I'm doing that? We can do without any mishaps in the middle of the search."

"Right."

She leapt to her feet, grabbed her tools and flew out of Surveillance.

I pursed my lips. "I must be getting old. The coffee doesn't taste that strong to me."

"Yes sir," said Nguyen.

Now I could see things beginning to fit together. I tried not to think of how Geoff would judge what I'd just done.

My securitati sergeants were quite capable of organizing the search so I could stay in Surveillance and brief them over the comm.

"And make sure they know we're looking for someone who's already sandbagged one man and thrown him over the side. They're to stay in groups of at least four and keep their trackers on."

Which meant that everyone who could have legitimately accessed that Rarden bay had three pairs of eyes and a tracking device to snitch on them if they got up to anything other than searching.

I drank my coffee slowly, hiding my jangling nerves from Nguyen. If the search came up blank, I was back to square one with no clue where to look for square two.

The weather did me a favor by deteriorating. Every camera viewing an external window showed the horizon at a different angle, none of which agreed with my inner ear. I tried not to look at them. If Nguyen thought I looked tense, he'd think it was because I was bracing myself to stay in my seat.

Nguyen looked pale enough that he probably wasn't paying attention to my body language. He hadn't experienced the corkscrew motion of the *Ayn Rand* in a heavy sea before, but he assured me he could look after Surveillance.

The call came from the lifeboat deck. I took the lift up and stepped outside the superstructure into a hail of freezing salt spray. Why did it have to be the side of the ship facing the wind? I worked my way along the rail to the two securitati standing by a lifeboat.

"In here, sir!"

I recognized Martinez's voice from inside the parka. He unhooked the lifeboat's tarpaulin rope from enough cleats that I could duck under it without the tarpaulin blowing away.

The benches looked as spartan as they must have done on the *Titanic's* boats. The idea of McNamara or the Yefimovs spending a few days in it cheered me up a bit.

I panned my torch, sending the shadows of the benches zig-zagging across the hull until I found the rifle lying against a case of survival gear. I didn't have McNamara's knowledge of antique weapons, but I knew the mechanism above the breach belonged to a flintlock rather than anything modern.

It was bigger than the evidence bags I'd brought with me, so I sent Martinez for a rubbish bag and crouched in the shelter of the boat. While I was waiting, I called Fern and asked to use her workshop to examine it.

"Any problems with the cameras?" I asked her once I got there.

"No. But it could have been in the boat awhile, couldn't it?"

Not unless the last search had been very lax indeed.

I said, "Maybe."

I put on a pair of nitrile gloves and eased the weapon out of the bag. I walked around the bench, looking closely without touching it.

"What is it?" asked Fern.

"It didn't come from our armory, that's for sure. No rifling... See the crest of arms on the stock?"

"That's our royal family, isn't it?"

"Yes, from the days before KingCorp bought them out. Royal Armouries. Unless I'm very much mistaken, this is a land pattern musket, standard issue for the British Army for most of the eighteenth and nineteenth centuries. Brown Bess to her friends. More to the point are those not-so-brown stains around the butt."

London gangs sometimes used antiques as collateral. Hard men tended to prefer antiques made to go bang than to look decorative, so I'd met Brown Bess before. She was rare enough to be valuable, but easy enough to find if you had the cash.

"Blood?"

"Looks like it."

"Kurata's?"

I didn't answer. I dusted the stock and barrel for fingerprints.

"Nothing," I said. "Still, we know who's got a predilection for antique weapons and a problem with Kurata."

"McNamara?"

"Yes. McNamara." I photographed the prints. "I'll see if I can get one of the infirmary techs to match the DNA in the bloodstains with a swab from Kurata's penthouse."

"They can do that?

I put the musket back in the bag and shrugged.

"I expect so. They use DNA to test for diseases, don't they? It's the same principle."

I doubted it. The *Ayn Rand*'s infirmary was as well-equipped as a shipload of ageing trillionaires demanded, but matching human DNA between samples wasn't the same as diagnosing an infection.

"We don't need to wait for that," I said. "We both know it will be Kurata's blood, don't we?"

"I guess. What are we going to do while we're not waiting?"

"Search the crew quarters. That's where we'll find the next piece of evidence."

"It is?"

"Yes. I'll brief the securitati in an hour. Before that, I need to take this to the infirmary and brief the captain."

"I'm not sure I understand, sir," said Nguyen. "Should we be concentrating on the cameras in the crew quarters or the superstructure?"

It didn't matter, but I wasn't going to tell him that.

"Crew quarters. Let's see if the search flushes anyone. I'll be back in a minute."

I left before Nguyen could say more, leaving him in Surveillance with Fern. If I was as close to the truth as I hoped, any lift I used would break down in an awkward enough place to keep me out of trouble for the next hour. I levered myself up a couple of swaying staircases to look out of a porthole. Gray sea rolled out of a haze of spray that would keep any self-respecting trillionaire off the deck. I could see a few hundred meters at most. So far, so good.

I returned to Surveillance and joined Nguyen and Fern watching securitati moving from cabin to cabin. One screen showed a woman chasing a securitati team out of a dorm. I couldn't hear her tirade, but her twisted features and pointing finger made me feel unclean.

One of the securitati turned and pointed back.

I spoke into my comm. "Leave it, Cissé. Concentrate on the job."

Cissé threw up his hands and entered another cabin. The woman shouted through the door.

Nguyen sat bolt upright. "Sir, we have another camera failure."

Right on time.

"Christ. Not again," I said.

Nguyen rattled off the dead circuits, which included two corridors between the crew quarters and the superstructure. I consulted a schematic and saw they were joined by twenty meters of cross-corridor.

"Shall we?" I asked Fern.

"You don't have to come. I can fix them on my own. Hadn't you better keep an eye on things here?"

"I'd like to see for myself. Nothing's going to happen on the working cameras, is it?"

I buckled my security belt with holsters for gun, taser and flexicuffs.

"Got your tools?"

I put an edge into my voice, sounding like I felt the situation slipping out of control. Fern watched me with her lips pressed into a bloodless line.

"After you," I said.

She hefted her toolbox. I followed her toward the elevators.

"Not the lifts," I said. "Who knows what might pack up next? Let's be old school and take the stairs."

She turned to argue. I took her elbow and guided her up the stairs ahead of me. Her shoulders were so taut they must have hurt. My gaze slid down to her backside. None the worse for the extra kilos she dressed to hide. I stamped on the thought. Sometimes my mind throws distractions at me when I need to be at my most focused.

Sometimes I disgust myself.

Fern turned toward the corridor at the top of the stairs.

"Let's start on the next deck up," I said.

"This deck's out too. I may as well start here."

Perhaps it was her vulnerability that made me want to touch her arm. It wasn't that she sounded as if she was desperately trying to keep the situation under control. It was that she'd thought it was under her control in the first place.

"Next deck up."

I used the voice that got smackheads into squad cars and committed anarchists to name their contacts. It got Fern up the stairs. She didn't even argue when I led her to the cross-corridor I'd seen on the schematic. She shifted her weight from foot to foot.

"What are we doing here?" she asked. "There's no camera circuits here."

"I know there aren't. That's not why we're here, is it?"

"I don't know what you mean."

"Yes, you do. You've been trying to get me anywhere but here. You see, I meant it when I said I knew who did it."

I had to keep talking. If her attention was on what I was saying, it wasn't on what to do about it.

"What I didn't know was who was behind it. You or any of the senior techies would know which cameras to blow, but hacking the Rarden bay took some skill. I'm impressed with that."

"No!"

"You'll be happy to know that telling me about McNamara's loan almost worked. I liked him for it until I saw how you reacted to Kurata's calls on Lydia Yefimova. You made excuses for him when there was no reason to look past the bleeding obvious reason for him to be sneaking into her room. Why would you care if he was screwing around? And if you had a reason to care, why weren't you bothered when we found it was him who went over the side? The bleeding obvious covered the first, which made the second more interesting: You knew he was still alive.

"That's why I had Nguyen watch the superstructure during the search. It was an experiment. When I said I knew who did it, you couldn't know if I meant McNamara. You'd have to make sure. So I made sure I knew where everyone else with access to the Rardens was and sent you out on your own, knowing where was and wasn't being watched. I had a little bet with myself that evidence against McNamara would turn up where Nguyen wasn't watching.

"The Brown Bess was going a bit too far. Antique weapons are McNamara's obsession. He'd never bounce Kurata's head off one. And if he did and needed to get rid of it, why chuck it in a lifeboat instead of over the side?"

"What are you saying? Someone threw Tanjiro Kurata overboard. You saw it happen."

"No, I saw someone throw something human-looking over the side. With the wide-angle lens and the low light, I couldn't see whether it was Kurata or a few sheets and pillows sewn together. Am I right?"

She looked away.

"Which answers the question that started bothering me from the moment I started thinking about it properly. Well, as soon as I got some sleep anyway.

"Why was the camera in the Rarden bay still working? The ditcher took out every other camera he had to pass. Why leave the one that showed the actual murder? If we hadn't seen it, we wouldn't have called the securitati, and he'd have had hours to get rid of any evidence. It only makes sense if throwing Kurata overboard was less important than making us think he'd thrown Kurata overboard. A murderer wouldn't want to film the murder. An amateur faking a murder might."

By now, most people would be crying, screaming at me, perhaps throwing punches. It must have cost Fern an enormous effort to keep her face so blank.

"I guess you've been hiding him in your cabin, which is about to be searched. He's going to have to get out, and the obvious place to go is his penthouse. It's not as if there's anyone else using it, is there? You should have blown every camera on the ship. That way I'd have had the whole ship to search for him. But if you did that, I'd have to wonder why the ditcher didn't do it to cover the murder and then I'd wonder about that camera in the Rarden bay, wouldn't I? You were far enough ahead of me to know what I'd make of it if I got thinking about it. So you blew the cameras in what looked like random places but which gave him a clear route from the crew quarters to his penthouse. But your random route only left him one cross-corridor he could use."

I was speaking quietly, with long enough pauses to listen. Right on cue, I heard footsteps approaching.

"Keep quiet," I whispered, "or someone will get hurt."

That got a reaction. Her expression prompted me to draw my taser.

"I mean it."

I put my back to the wall and sidled toward the junction with the corridor the footsteps were coming down.

The *Ayn Rand* mocked my ambush with a lurch that threw the walker into me. I staggered.

Tanjiro Kurata looked at me, then Fern.

"Run!" shouted Fern.

Oh what the hell? I tasered him. How often would I get to do that to a guest?

He was still twitching when I got the flexicuffs on him. I expected Fern to run before I could replace the cartridge, but she knelt and cradled Kurata's head.

"Tanjiro, darling, please speak to me."

I shook my head. "You can't be serious. Can't you see he stitched you up?"

"We're in *love*, you smug bastard."

"Oh, come on, he was using you. Don't tell me you thought you were going to live in luxury and make babies together. He'd chuck you as soon as you got him ashore…"

She leapt at me, bouncing punches and kicks off me. She couldn't have been in a fight since the school playground. I had her against the wall in a full Nelson before she raised a bruise.

"Mr. Harme, I presume? Captain Espinosa did not mention you had such a way with women."

I looked round to see a woman leading two large men. Her bow did nothing to dilute her air of not-to-be-messed-with. It fit her as well as her white uniform.

"Warrant Officer Sayako Itoh," she introduced herself. "Japanese Maritime Self Defense Force."

She spoke over Fern's obscenities.

"You were supposed to wait until I called you," I said.

"I know, and I thank you for your invitation. But I heard noise and thought you might need assistance. I see I was mistaken."

"I think I've got it covered."

Fern ran out of breath and out of fight. She felt as though she was deflating under my grip.

"Fern," I said, "can I trust you not to do anything stupid if I let you go?"

"Go to hell."

"Fern?"

"Yes, okay."

As soon as I released her, she was back to cradling Kurata's head. "Tanjiro, Tanjiro, speak to me."

"That counts as stupid," I said.

Kurata groaned.

I turned to Itoh. "How was your flight?"

"Down to your helideck from five thousand feet in this weather? Bumpy, but our pilot has not enjoyed himself so much in years. I doubt anyone but your bridge crew saw us come in. You asked us to collect the murderer of Tanjiro Kurata. This is him?"

"Slight change of plan. This is Tanjiro Kurata himself, fully recovered from being murdered. Given that he faked it, it wasn't much of a trick."

Itoh knelt beside Fern, studying Kurata's face.

"Well, well." Itoh sounded as though her lottery numbers had come up.

"Quite," I said. "Now I suggest you get him off the *Ayn Rand* and into Japanese jurisdiction before anyone else notices his little miracle. I've got the securitati searching cabins at the other end of the ship, so they shouldn't get in your way."

Itoh gave an order in Japanese. Her men hauled Kurata to his feet.

"Harme, call your securitati," said Kurata. "Make these men release me."

Itoh looked at me with a non-commissioned officer's reverence for a direct order. Formidable as they were, she and her two men wouldn't get past the securitati.

"Did he say something?" I asked her.

She looked relieved. "I don't think so."

"They sometimes mumble when they've been tasered. Nothing worth paying attention to."

Fern leapt off her knees. "He just ordered you to — "

"Fern! I told you not to do anything stupid," I said.

"You stupid bitch!" Kurata regained his wits, if not his manners. "You said you'd killed the cameras."

Fern looked as though he'd slapped her. He probably would have done if he wasn't cuffed. "I did, Tanjiro, my love, I did everything we planned —"

"You did nothing. You screwed it all up."

I exchanged an eyeroll with Itoh.

"His accomplice?" Itoh had no difficulty in raising her voice over Kurata's invective. She sounded capable of shouting over a typhoon, and probably had done.

"She's committed no crime in Japanese jurisdiction. I'd like to be more hospitable, but…"

Once Kurata finished reaming Fern out, he'd turn to me. I couldn't keep pretending I hadn't heard his orders.

"Of course." Itoh took the hint. "On behalf of Japan, I thank you."

She bowed again.

Fern's jaw dangled as she watched them haul Kurata away. His fury had knocked her senseless.

"Now you know," I said. "I could've ordered you to stay in Surveillance, but I wanted you to see he'd played you."

"He loved me." Her voice was hardly above a whisper.

"No, he didn't. His family must have warned him that frigate was coming, which would have been about a week ago. Was it about then that he suddenly discovered he was in love with you?"

"Bastard."

I took that as a yes.

"What really pisses me off is that he was about to get the whole crew beached in Murmansk. Did you know about that?"

"What? No."

I believed her. She was in no state to lie convincingly.

"One call. That's all it would have taken. One call to tell his family he was alive, and we'd all have been off the hook."

"We couldn't make a call. You might have been listening in."

I couldn't argue with that.

"So, you'd hide him while I chased McNamara, and he'd keep telling you he loved you, till the Kuratas' goons met us in Murmansk. Then you'd suddenly find you'd outlived your usefulness. Whatever he promised was no more to him than a line of code is to you. How you tell a mechanism what to do."

"You're finished. When he tells his family what you did..."

"I'll be put ashore and never work for the rich again. I know. But nobody else will be punished. Perhaps I deserve it for all I've done for people like him and McNamara and Yefimov. I never thought of myself as building and protecting their world, but it's what I've spent my life doing. I should be grateful to that little toe-rag for giving me the opportunity to say 'no more'. Now I have a favor to ask."

"A favor? For *you*?"

"All that information you lifted from Kurata's computer? I can think of someone who might appreciate it."

"Bastard."

I guessed she meant Kurata as much as me. I hid a smile. She was angry enough with Kurata to give me the information. When I'd got back to London from wherever they put me ashore and gave the data to Geoff's dissident friends, my son might have a reason to be proud of me.

Keep reading for the opening pages of *Caresaway*, DJ Cockburn's novelette about a dedicated scientist who develops a drug that can cure depression, but perhaps destroyed the world in the process.

If there was a pill that made you successful, would you take it?

What if it also made you a psychopath?

Edward Crofte strode through the door marked 'CEO' without knocking. He'd been looking forward to doing that for a long time. He stood in the middle of the room until Anthony D'Olivera looked up from the papers he was packing into a box.

Back in the bad old days, Edward would have been able to interpret D'Olivera's expression instantly. Now he was less certain, but as long as he could see defeat, he knew all he needed to.

"Come to mark your new territory?" D'Olivera's Cape Flats accent, normally no more than a hint in his vowels, was clear even to Edward's English ears.

Edward strolled to the plate glass window where he looked down at Buitengracht Street, carving through Cape Town toward the cloud pouring off Table Mountain like some impossibly huge waterfall. An open-topped Maserati turned left out of Buitengracht on to Strand Street. With his CEO's salary, he'd be able to afford one for himself. Or at least persuade the bank to extend his credit far enough.

"Come on, Anthony," he said. "It's not like that. Most of our profit comes from Caresaway, so you can't blame the board if they think you're holding up the marketing."

Edward didn't look around, but he could feel D'Olivera's eyes on the back of his neck.

"And Caresaway's your baby, right?" asked D'Olivera.

"Well yes, actually, it is." That might have been a gloat too far. "Though of course, it was you who brought it on board. And me with it."

"Hm." D'Olivera's single syllable carried years of regret. He couldn't know the details of the boardroom alliance Edward had built against him, but twenty minutes ago he'd felt the result in the no-confidence vote.

"We're in the middle of a global recession, Anthony. We need to make the most of our one blockbuster product."

"So you said in the board meeting. Repeatedly. But does it bother you that the product may be *why* we're in the middle of a global recession?"

"No."

Edward turned at D'Olivera's sigh.

"Do you remember who you used to be, Edward?" asked D'Olivera. "The day you told me about Caresaway?"

"I was a failure. A victim. Now I'm a CEO. Works for me."

"You struck me as a man of ideals and compassion. You genuinely wanted Caresaway to help people."

"It has. I've given the world its only effective antidepressant. It's helped a lot of people. If I've done well out of it, I've earned it."

"But you never meant it to become a corporate aid, did you? Now everyone who wants to make it in business is popping them like they used to snort cocaine. Look at you. You were the first to kill your soul with the stuff. Now you stand there smirking, but we both know this isn't really you."

Edward rolled his eyes at the metaphysical nonsense. If he'd ever had a soul, whatever that was, it hadn't been doing him much good.

"Believe what you like, Anthony," he said. "It may help you adjust to retirement."

D'Olivera turned away. Very few people could match gazes with Edward Crofte. A couple of seconds was all it took them to recognize the power behind his eyes. Making people look away was one of the little pleasures that made it worth getting out of bed in the morning.

A knock sounded on the door.

"Come in," said Edward, before D'Olivera could react.

Beatrice Tshabalala, D'Olivera's PA, sidled in as though she feared stepping on a snake hiding in the carpet.

"Anthony? We've just heard," she said. "I'm so sorry."

"Thank you, Beatrice," said D'Olivera.

She hugged him. As she stepped away, she darted a look at Edward. Edward met her eyes. She looked away, so she didn't see him sneer. Her creaseless trouser suit, her immaculate cornrows, her understated makeup - everything about her screamed 'take me seriously' - but one glance was enough to tell her where the power in the room lay. She could try to hide from it in the sentimental look she was sharing with D'Olivera but she knew. Prey could always recognize a predator.

"Anthony, I've sent someone to get some drinks in. We'd really like you to join us when you've finished," she said.

"Thank you, Beatrice. That's very thoughtful," said D'Olivera. "I'll come down now. I'm sure Edward isn't in such a hurry to move in, and the company downstairs would be a little more to my liking."

Cheeky sod. Still, no harm in a show of magnanimity.

"Go right ahead," Edward said. "As long as I can move my stuff in by tomorrow morning."

D'Olivera and Beatrice walked into the open-plan admin office outside the CEO's office. People left their desks to shake D'Olivera's hand and follow him to the drinks party. This must be what a lion felt watching a herd of wildebeest.

Edward noticed an anomaly. The pretty blond intern was deviating from the herd and moving in his direction. Lisa, that was her name.

She stopped at the open door and put a hand on it as though it was a physical barrier. Her hips swayed, revealing both her nervousness and her confidence that she could always get by with the right look at the right person. If he hadn't already slept with her, Edward would have found it irresistible. As he'd already had her a couple of times, it was merely tempting.

"Hi," she said.

He said nothing.

"I've just heard. It's wonderful news."

"Yes, thank you." Her smile didn't quite hit the confident flirting she was aiming for. Edward frowned to make it more difficult for her. It might be amusing to see how hard she'd try.

"Does that mean you'll take me to a more expensive restaurant tonight?" she asked.

Full marks for effort. But why not? She had that brand of luscious you could only find in well-to-do girls who were still experimenting with adulthood. It withered away by the time they hit twenty-three or twenty-four.

"I'll pick you up at seven," he said. "But for now, you'd better go for drinks with everyone else."

"Okay. See you then."

She was, after all, one of the herd. In a week or so, she wouldn't even be that. She'd fade to bland after another date or two, and he understood safe sex at work. Only with temps and interns who could be fired without repercussion when he got bored with them.

He sat in D'Olivera's high-backed chair and put his feet up on the desk. Childish? Perhaps, but he was going to enjoy this office. He'd have to get rid of this chair and change the carpet; let people know the new regime would be different. No more first naming in here. He'd be Doctor Crofte or there'd be trouble.

No whining about killing souls and who he used to be when he didn't have a high-backed chair, which was what mattered. He'd been a pretty sorry specimen when he met D'Olivera, but that was a blip. It was absurd to think he'd made it here because of a few pills, even if they were his own invention. A man like him would always find his own level.

He could stop taking the pills right now and he'd still be Doctor Edward Crofte, inventor of Caresaway and CEO of Pharmakaap. Not Ed the unshaven of the drafty flat somewhere near

Cambridge. D'Olivera had talked as though he were addicted, like the miserable wrecks on the streets, their lives devoted to the next puff of tik. He took the blister pack of Caresaway out of his pocket and threw it in the waste basket. He felt no need to retrieve it. He wasn't an addict. He could never take another Caresaway pill and he'd still belong in the high-backed chair. Never be the pathetic excuse for a man he'd been the day he met D'Olivera.

Learn more about *Caresaway* and find purchase links at annorlundabooks.com/ caresaway

About the Author

DJ Cockburn is a British author with stories in Apex, Interzone, and various anthologies. His story "Beside the Damned River" won the 2014 James White Award. He has supported his unfortunate writing habit through medical research on various parts of the African continent and drinking a lot of coffee.

Earlier phases of his life have included teaching possibly unlucky children and experimenting on definitely unlucky fish. He can be found online at cockburndj.wordpress.com and has occasionally been caught twittering as @DJ_Cockburn.

About the Publisher

Annorlunda Books is a small press that publishes books to inform, entertain, and make you think. We publish short books (novella length or shorter) and collections of short writing, fiction and non-fiction.

Find more information about us and our books online: annorlundaenterprises.com/books or on Twitter: @AnnorlundaInc.

To stay up to date on all of our releases, subscribe to our mailing list at:

annorlundaenterprises.com/mailing-list

Selected Other Titles from Annorlunda Books

Short eBooks

Caresaway, by DJ Cockburn, a near future "inside your head" thriller about a scientist who discovers a cure for depression, but finds that it comes at a terrible cost.

Tattoo, by Michelle Rene, a novella about a young woman who appears in a cynical post-Judgement Day age, and the band of strangers who find themselves called to keep her safe.

Water into Wine, by Joyce Chng, a sci-fi novella about a family trying to build a life amidst an interstellar war that threatens everything.

The Burning, by J.P. Seewald, a novella set in the coal country of Pennsylvania, about a family struggling to cope as a slow-moving catastrophe threatens everything they have.

The Lilies of Dawn, by Vanessa Fogg, is a lyrical fantasy novelette about love, duty, family, and one young woman's coming of age.

The Inconvenient God, by Francesca Forrest, is a fantasy novelette about a government official tasked with retiring a god who isn't quite ready to leave.

Okay, So Look, by Micah Edwards, is a humorous, yet accurate and thought-provoking, retelling of the Book of Genesis.

Don't Call It Bollywood, by Margaret E. Redlich, is an introduction to the world of Hindi film.

The Dodo Knight, by Michelle Rene, is a novella about the friendship between Lewis Carroll and Alice Liddell, the muse for *Alice in Wonderland*.

Unspotted, by Justin Fox, is the story of the Cape Mountain Leopard and the author's own journey to try to see one.

Collections

Both Sides of My Skin, by Elizabeth Trach, a collection of short stories exploring the reality of pregnancy and motherhood.

Love and Other Happy Endings is a Taster Flight collectionof classic stories, all of which end on a high note.

Missed Chances is another Taster Flight of classic stories about love and "the one that got away."

Small and Spooky is a Taster Flight of classic ghost stories, all of which feature a child.

Hemmed In, a Taster Flight collection of classic short stories about women's lives.

Academaze, by Sydney Phlox, is a collection of essays and cartoons about life in academia